This book belongs to:

. . . .

Tiny Creatures

Peppa and George are helping
Grandpa Pig to pick vegetables.

Grandpa Pig hands Peppa a lettuce.

Peppa can see something sitting
on the lettuce.
"There's a horrible monster!"
she snorts.

"That's just a little snail!"
says Grandpa Pig.
"Grrr. Mon-sta!" says George.

George likes the snail.
Suddenly the snail disappears.

"Where's he gone?" asks Peppa.
"He's hiding in his shell,"
explains Grandpa Pig.

"Grandpa! George and I want to be snails," says Peppa.

"Well," says Grandpa Pig,
"these baskets can be your shells!"
"I'm going to eat up all Grandpa's
lettuces!" Peppa laughs.

Here are Peppa and George's friends.
"Can we be snails, too?" they ask.
"Well . . ." says Grandpa Pig.

"You could be something else exciting from the garden."
"What's that buzzing sound?" asks Peppa.

"It's coming from that little house,"
says Suzy.
"It's a bee house," explains Grandpa Pig.
"It's called a hive."

"The bees collect nectar from flowers and then fly to the hive to make it into honey."

"Hmmmm, I like honey," says Peppa.
"Let's pretend to be bees! Buzz! Buzz!
Buzz! Hee! Hee! Hee!"

"What busy bees!" laughs
Grandpa Pig.

Granny Pig has been baking bread.
"Would you busy bees like some
toast?" she asks.

"Yes please!" say Peppa and her friends.
"With lots of honey!"

"I like being a bee because they make lots of lovely honey!" says Suzy.

"I like being a snail," snorts
Peppa, "because they eat all of
Grandpa's vegetables!"

My
Family
Tree